THERE'S A ZOMBIE IN MY TREEHOUSE!

WORDS BY

KEN PLUME
AND
JOHN ROBINSON

ART BY

LEN PERALTA

THERE'S A ZOMBIE IN MY TREEHOUSE!

ISBN: 978-0-557-28932-5

Published by SPACE! Guys
4480-H S. Cobb Drive, PMB 394
Smyrna GA 30080-6984
USA

Printed in the United States of America
http://www.zombieinmytreehouse.com

Life on Cameron Lane was as normal as normal could be.

There were normal houses and normal families and normal cars in normal garages with normal trees in all the normal yards.

In this normal town, Johnny was a perfectly normal boy. You'd never guess there was anything particularly special about him, judging by his normal looks and normal demeanor. In fact, he was just a normal boy.

What wasn't normal, however, was the tree in his yard. Well, not the tree, really - it was just a normal tree. It wasn't even the treehouse nestled in its lofty limbs - that was normal, too.

On normal days, Johnny would come home after school and play in the treehouse. Some days, he'd rescue a princess from the evil dragon that perched menacingly in the topmost heights of the old oak tree. Other days, he'd vanquish the dread pirate lord whose flagship just happened to look suspiciously like the shed in Old Man Johnson's yard. Sometimes he even managed to save the Ruby Galaxy from the monstrous Zorggo - when his mother didn't make him come in too early.

There came a day, however, not that long ago, when Johnny found something abnormal in his normal life. It was the day that Johnny discovered...

A zombie! In HIS treehouse!

How was he supposed to play today – or ANY day?!? No matter how much he wanted to drive the Burly Bandits from Gruesome Gulch or defeat the Gray Hand Ninja Clan, with the presence of this undead intruder it certainly seemed like there was no way he'd ever be able to play in his treehouse again.

Things went from bad to worse when that bully Billy Davis from down the street stopped him while he was walking home from school. "Whatsamatter?" Billy the bully asked, "Why aren't you playing in your stupid little treehouse?"

"I can't go play in my treehouse," Johnny said. "There's a zombie in it."

"There's no such thing as a zombie, you ninny," Billy said.

"Well, if you think that, YOU can go tell him. He's right up in the treehouse.
I bet he'd love to hear he's not real. But I wouldn't do it, if I were you. You'd
have to be pretty stupid to do that."

"YOU'RE stupid! I'll go tell your imaginary zombie whatever I want," Billy
said with a sneer, then pushed Johnny out of the way.

And up the ladder he went.

And Johnny waited...

but Billy the bully never came back down again.

The next day, Johnny's sister interrupted him while he was sitting in the den. He was trying in vain to find something worth watching on television, unable to shake the feeling that the dread arch-pirate Ernie Black was now ruling the oceans in his absence. "What's wrong with you?" his sister asked. "Why aren't you out in your treehouse pretending you're a cowboy or a princess, or whatever it is you do out there?"

"I can't go pretend in my treehouse," Johnny said. "There's a zombie in it."

"That's silly. There can't be a zombie in your treehouse. Zombies can't climb trees," his sister said. "Everybody knows that."

"Well, everybody but this zombie, apparently. Because he's up in the treehouse. You're more than welcome to go tell him he can't possibly be up there. But I wouldn't, if I were you."

"I think I will go tell him," his sister said, smirking.

And up the ladder she went.

And Johnny waited...

and waited...

but his sister never came back down again.

The next day, Johnny's mother came into his room while he was lying in his bed, wondering what he was going to do now that he didn't have a treehouse anymore. Who would save the Queen of the Moon?

"What's wrong, Johnny?" his mother asked. "Why aren't you up in your treehouse having an adventure as a secret agent or something?"

"I can't go have any more adventures in my treehouse," Johnny said. "There's a zombie in it."

"Now dear, we've talked about this before. Zombies aren't real. They're legends. In reality, they're just people who THINK they've died and been brought back from the grave," his mother said. "They don't know any better. Perhaps it's just a confused person in your treehouse."

"Well, the zombie in my treehouse definitely doesn't know any better, because he's real and he's up there right now. It'd be great if someone could un-confuse him so he'd go away. But I wouldn't do it, if I were you."

"Nonsense! I will go tell that poor, deluded man right this instant," his mother said.

And up the ladder she went.

And Johnny waited...

and waited...

and waited...

but his mother never came back down again.

The next day, Johnny's father came into the kitchen while Johnny was sitting at the breakfast table, building the Great Pyramid out of cookies.

"Johnny, why are you moping about in here?" his father asked. "And have you seen your mother and sister?"

Johnny sighed. "I'm in here because I can't go up in my treehouse and play. There's a zombie in it. And Mom and Sis went up to go take care of him."

"Hmmm," his father said. "Well, I hope they remember that it takes a nice strong blow to the head to stop a zombie. And really, if it's only one zombie, he should be easy enough to deal with. I'm surprised and a little disappointed you weren't able to solve this problem on your own."

"Well, he seemed to be more than I could handle, Dad, because he's still up in the treehouse. Maybe you could show me how to do it, so I could have my treehouse back. I'd be sure to take notes so I could handle the next one. But maybe you should get some help, just in case."

"Oh, poppycock, son. If it's only one zombie, I won't need anyone else! Dad'll show you how it's done, straightaway," his father said, as he grabbed a sledgehammer.

And up the ladder he went.

And Johnny waited...

and waited...

and waited...

and waited...

but his father never came back down again.

Johnny is **still** waiting for someone who can help him with his zombie problem. Because although it's nice to have the bully gone, and he does miss his mother and his father and his sister (mostly)...

He really, really misses his treehouse.

7240107R0

Made in the USA
Lexington, KY
02 November 2010